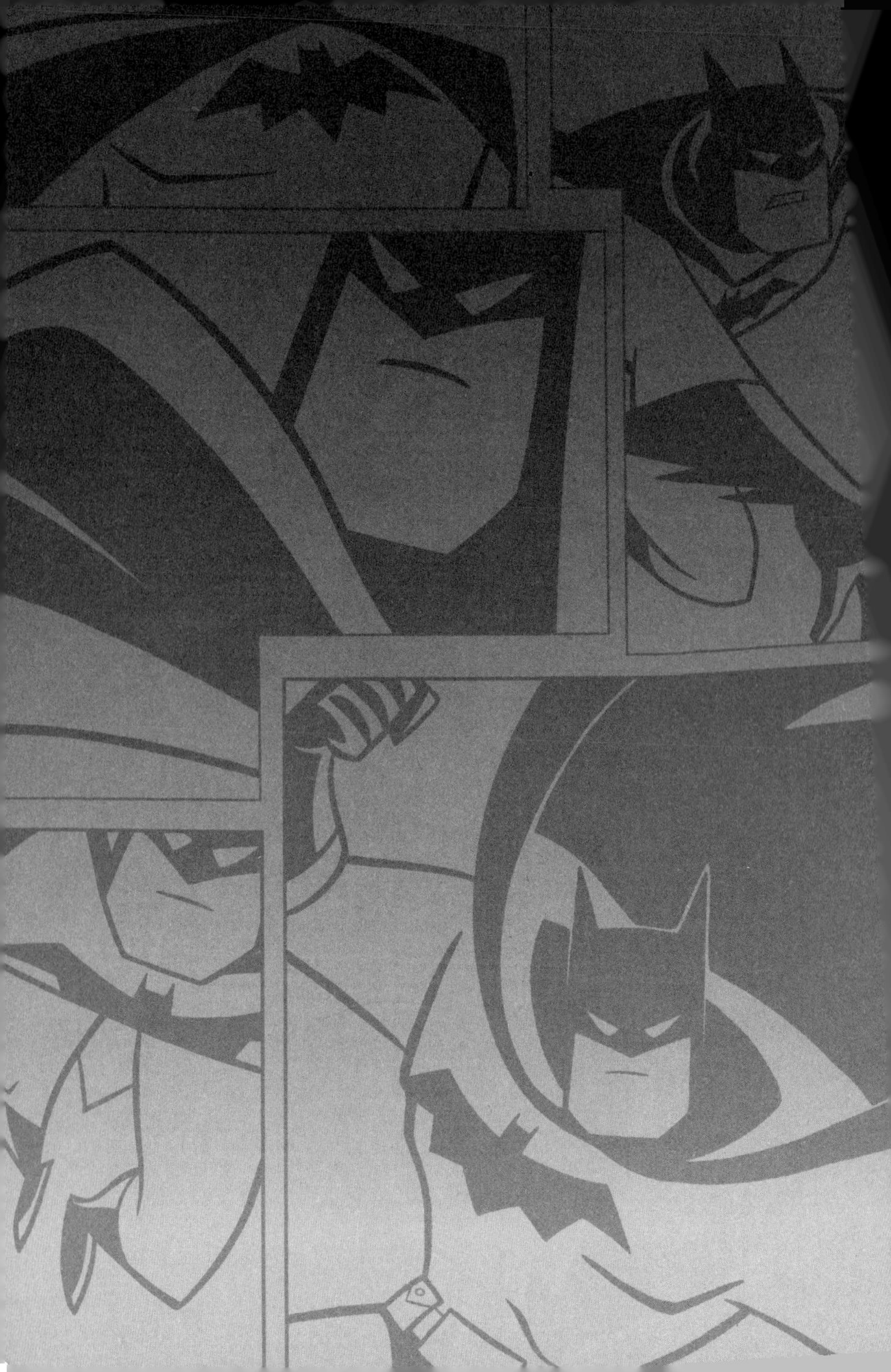

SUPER DC HEROES

BATMAN

Emperor OF THE AIRWAVES

WRITTEN BY
DONALD LEMKE

ILLUSTRATED BY
ERIK DOESCHER,
MIKE DeCARLO, AND
LEE LOUGHRIDGE

BATMAN CREATED BY
BOB KANE

STONE ARCH BOOKS
MINNEAPOLIS · SAN DIEGO

Published by Stone Arch Books in 2009
151 Good Counsel Drive, P.O. Box 669
Mankato, Minnesota 56002
www.stonearchbooks.com

Library of Congress Cataloging-in-Publication Data
Lemke, Donald B.
    Emperor of the Airwaves / by Donald Lemke; illustrated by Erik
Doescher.
    p. cm. — (DC Super Heroes. Batman)
    ISBN 978-1-4342-1153-8 (library binding)
    ISBN 978-1-4342-1364-8 (pbk.)
    [1. Superheroes—Fiction.] I. Doescher, Erik, ill. II. Title.
PZ7.L53746Emp 2009
[Fic]—dc22   2008032443

Summary: The Penguin purchases Gotham's largest media company.
Meanwhile, a crime wave hits the city. Batman soon learns that these events
are related. After the Dark Knight stops a crime, the Penguin's TV news
channel edit the security tapes and police reports to make Batman look
like a criminal. People begin to fear the Dark Knight. If he can't prove his
innocence, the hero will end up in prison, and the Penguin will fly free.

Art Director: Bob Lentz
Designer: Brann Garvey

1 2 3 4 5 6 14 13 12 11 10 09

TABLE OF CONTENTS

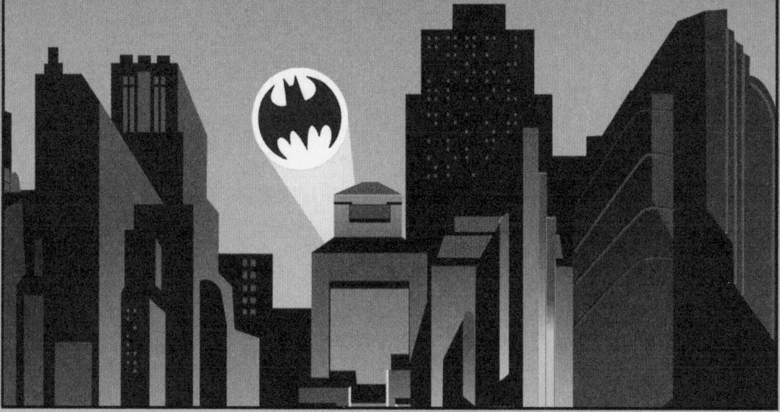

CHAPTER 1

THE EVENING NEWS

On the first night of spring, a cold, wet snow fell onto the Wayne Manor courtyard. Inside the grand mansion, billionaire Bruce Wayne settled into his chair. He took the final sip of his nightly tea, picked up the television remote, and flicked on the news.

"Another cold night in Gotham City," reported anchor Spring O'Hara. "Later in the weather forecast, we'll tell you about a possible warm-up headed our way . . ."

"A welcomed change. Wouldn't you say, Master Bruce?" said a voice from the door.

Bruce looked over his shoulder. Alfred, his loyal butler, entered the room. "I'll believe it when I see it," Bruce said. "These reporters never get anything right." He turned down the volume on the television. "I hope the noise didn't wake you, Alfred."

"Not at all, sir," said Alfred. "I just came by to offer you another spot of tea." The butler placed a silver serving tray on the table. He held up a steaming teapot and began pouring before Bruce could reply.

"Thanks, Alfred," said Bruce. "Anything to get rid of this chill."

"Yes," Alfred said. "Although this chill may be ridding us of another problem."

Alfred pointed toward the television. On the screen, Bruce saw the headline in bold letters: **GOTHAM CRIME RATE DECREASES.**

Bruce reached for the remote to turn the volume back up. Then suddenly, outside the frosted window, a spotlight shined through the darkened sky. In the bright beam of light was the symbol of a bat. Both men knew exactly what the Bat-Signal meant.

"What did I tell you, Alfred," said Bruce, quickly rising from his chair. "These reporters never get anything right." He turned and exited the room, heading toward the Batcave. The underground cavern contained the equipment he used as Batman, Gotham's greatest crime fighter.

Moments later, Alfred felt the loud rumble of an engine thunder beneath his feet. He looked outside the window. Through the falling snow, he watched the Batmobile speed away.

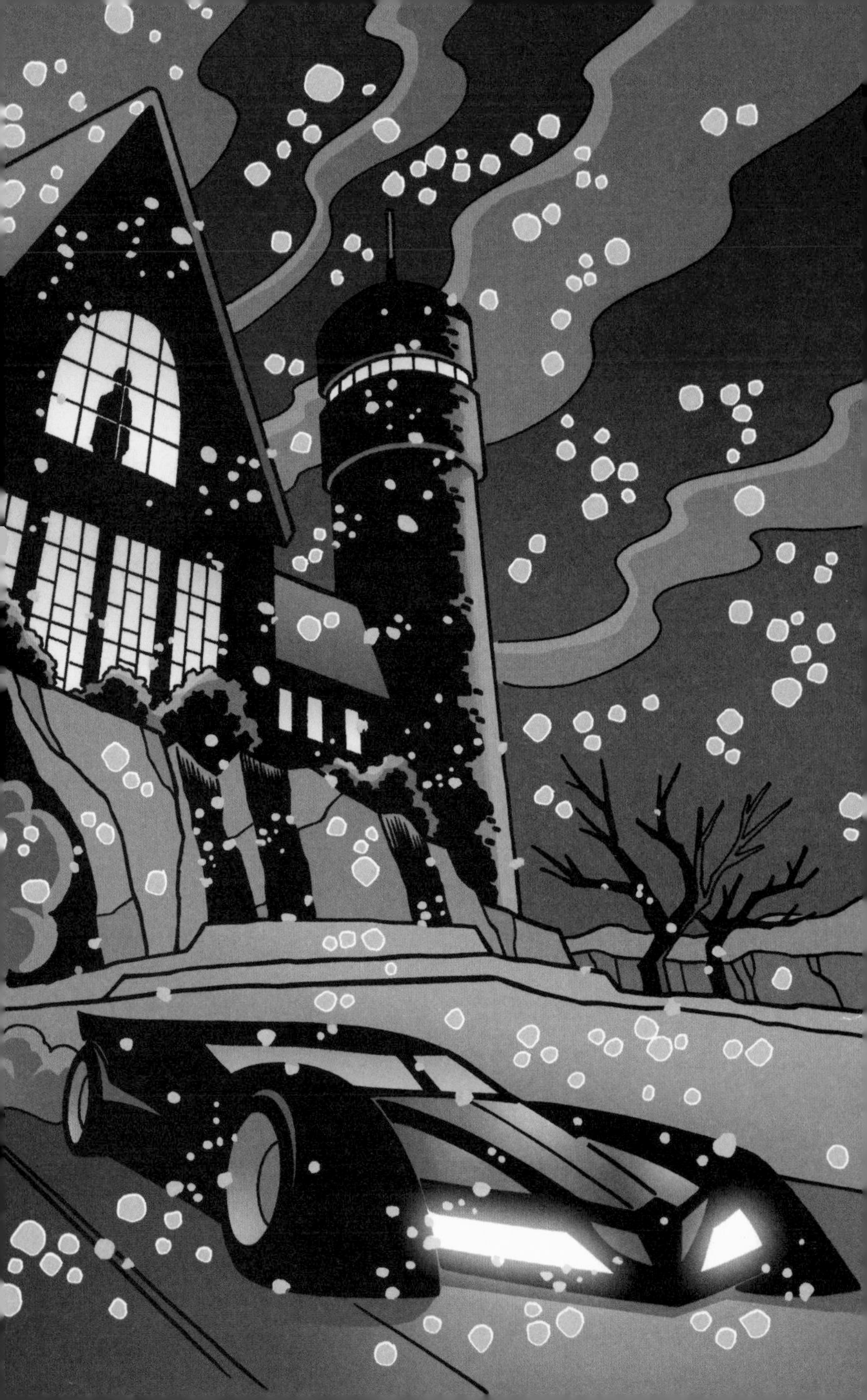

When the car's taillights had faded, Alfred returned to his duties. He stoked the fire and tidied up the room. Then, as he reached to turn off the television, Alfred saw a familiar face on the screen.

"Penguin," he said, cringing at the sight of the fowl-faced crook. "What's he up to this time?" Alfred turned up the volume to hear the news report.

". . . And finally tonight," O'Hara began, "WGBS Channel 12 has just been purchased by Oswald Cobblepot, wealthy owner of the Iceberg Lounge nightclub. The multi-million-dollar deal also includes the *Gotham Gazette* and WKGC radio station."

Alfred clicked off the television and stood for a moment in the darkened room. Unlike the weather forecast, he suspected this change would be anything but welcomed.

CHAPTER 2

ICE THIEF

Speeding toward Gotham City, Batman switched on the Batmobile's wireless system. He punched a button and speed-dialed Commissioner James Gordon. Although some members of the police force didn't trust the Caped Crusader, the commissioner always welcomed Batman's help.

"Where's the crime?" asked Batman, speaking into the car's wireless transmitter.

"Take your pick," Commissioner Gordon replied. "I've received silent alarms from more than a dozen jewelry stores."

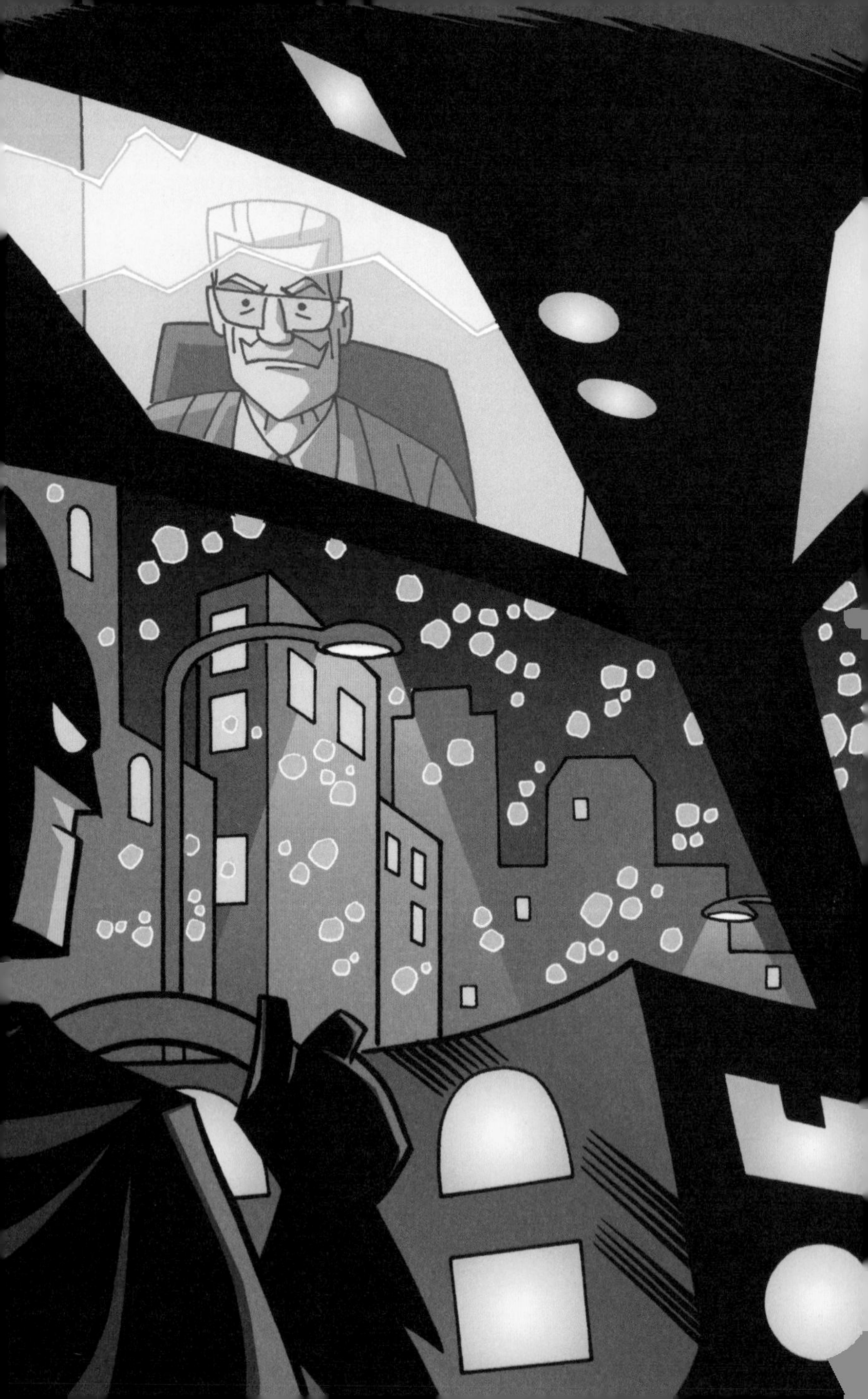

"Sounds like you've got a small crime wave starting," said Batman.

"More like a big problem," Gordon said. "My officers are completely outnumbered."

Batman switched on the Batmobile's afterburners. With a sudden jolt, the car quickly reached max speed. "Not anymore," said Batman.

Across town, a black van slid to a stop in front of Don's Diamond Store. The van's back doors quickly swung open. A tall man, wearing a black ski mask and carrying an automatic rifle, jumped out and rushed inside the store.

"Open the case, old man!" the thug yelled at the owner of the jewelry store. The criminal pointed his weapon at the glass counter filled with diamonds.

"Don't shoot!" the owner pleaded. He raised his hands into the air. "Take whatever you want!"

The thief handed him a large, green garbage bag. "Fill it up!" he shouted. "And make it quick!"

The store owner slowly lowered his arms. He leaned over the counter and took the bag with one hand. With the other hand, he secretly triggered the store's silent alarm button.

As the thief kept an eye on the front door, the owner filled the bag. Soon, it was overflowing with hundreds of valuable bracelets, rings, and necklaces.

"What's taking so long?" yelled the thief.

"Here!" said the owner, holding out the bag. "That's everything I have!"

The masked thug grabbed the bag. "You know the only thing I like more than a fresh coat of snow?" he asked, walking backwards toward the exit. "A bag full of ice!"

The crook raised the garbage bag filled with jewels into the air. He let out an evil laugh and spun quickly toward the exit. "What the —!" yelled the thug, surprised by what he saw.

In the store's doorway was a tall, shadowy figure. The masked man stood in silence, letting snow fall onto his long, black cape.

"Batman!" yelled the owner, recognizing the crime fighter. "He's stealing my jewels!"

Batman walked slowly toward the crook. "Hand over the diamonds," he growled.

The crook stumbled backward, clutching the bag of jewels even tighter. "Sorry, Batman," he said. "This bling belongs to a different bird." Then he pointed his weapon at the Caped Crusader. "But maybe you'd like some lead instead."

RAT-TAT-TAT! RAT-TAT-TAT! The crook's automatic rifle shook in a flurry of gunfire. Hot lead bullets spit from the barrel in quick bursts of flames.

Batman leapt and spun into the air. His long cape twirled like a helicopter blade, throwing off the fine powder of snow into the eyes of the thief. The cloud of frozen whiteness blinded the crook for a moment. Before he could recover, a large black boot struck him square in the chest.

"Oof!" The criminal flew backward across the room from Batman's kick.

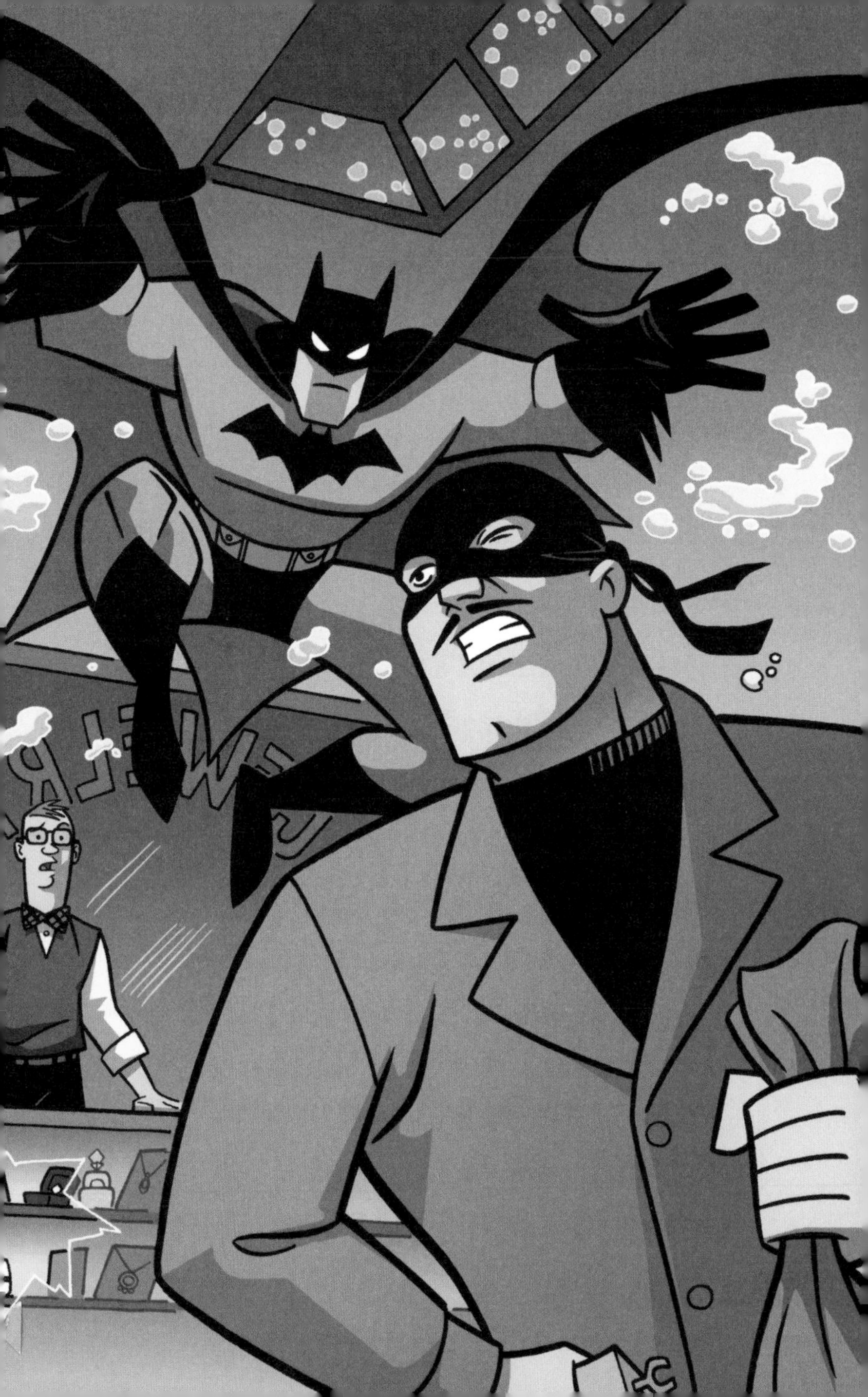

SMASH! He crashed into the empty display case near the store's cash register. The owner looked on, stunned. He watched Batman land as silent as snow and move toward the fallen criminal.

"The diamonds," Batman demanded, kneeling down and holding out his black leather glove.

The Dark Knight's powerful voice awakened the dazed crook. "Here! Take them! Just don't hurt me!" he whimpered, handing over the garbage bag.

Batman turned toward the store owner and held out the bag full of jewels. "I believe these belong to you," he said.

The owner reached out and grabbed the green bag, shaking with both fright and joy. "Thank you, Batman," he exclaimed.

The Dark Knight turned back toward the crook. Suddenly, the store windows lit up in a swirl of red and blue lights. Sirens echoed throughout room. The Gotham City Police had arrived.

Two officers in bulletproof vests burst through the doorway. "Freeze!" yelled one of the cops.

The crook scrambled out the store's back door like a frightened rat. Batman smiled at the officers, raising his hands into the air.

"You've caught me, boys," he said. "But if you'll excuse me, I have a criminal to catch."

Batman quickly spun toward the rear exit and fled into the night.

CHAPTER 3

AIR PENGUIN

Early the next morning, the Batmobile rumbled into the entrance of the Batcave. After removing the Batsuit, Bruce Wayne returned to the sitting room of Wayne Manor and settled into his evening chair. He took a sip from the cold cup of tea beside him on the table, grimaced, and then flicked on the television.

Reporter Spring O'Hara was back on the air. Below her on the screen, Bruce saw the morning headline: **BREAKING NEWS! THE BAT BURGLAR STRIKES!**

"Bat Burglar?!" said Bruce, puzzled.

"Moments ago, Channel 12 received a security tape from Don's Diamond Store, the scene of an attempted burglary last night," reported O'Hara. "It shows shocking evidence of a very unlikely suspect."

Bruce moved closer to the television and watched as the security tape began. In the fuzzy images, he saw a close-up of Batman. He was entering the doorway of Don's Diamond Store. "Hand over the diamonds," he growled from within the mask.

The sound of his own voice startled Bruce for a moment. But then, something startled him even more. The camera quickly switched to a close-up image of the store owner standing near the cash register. "Take whatever you want," the owner screamed, raising his hands into the air.

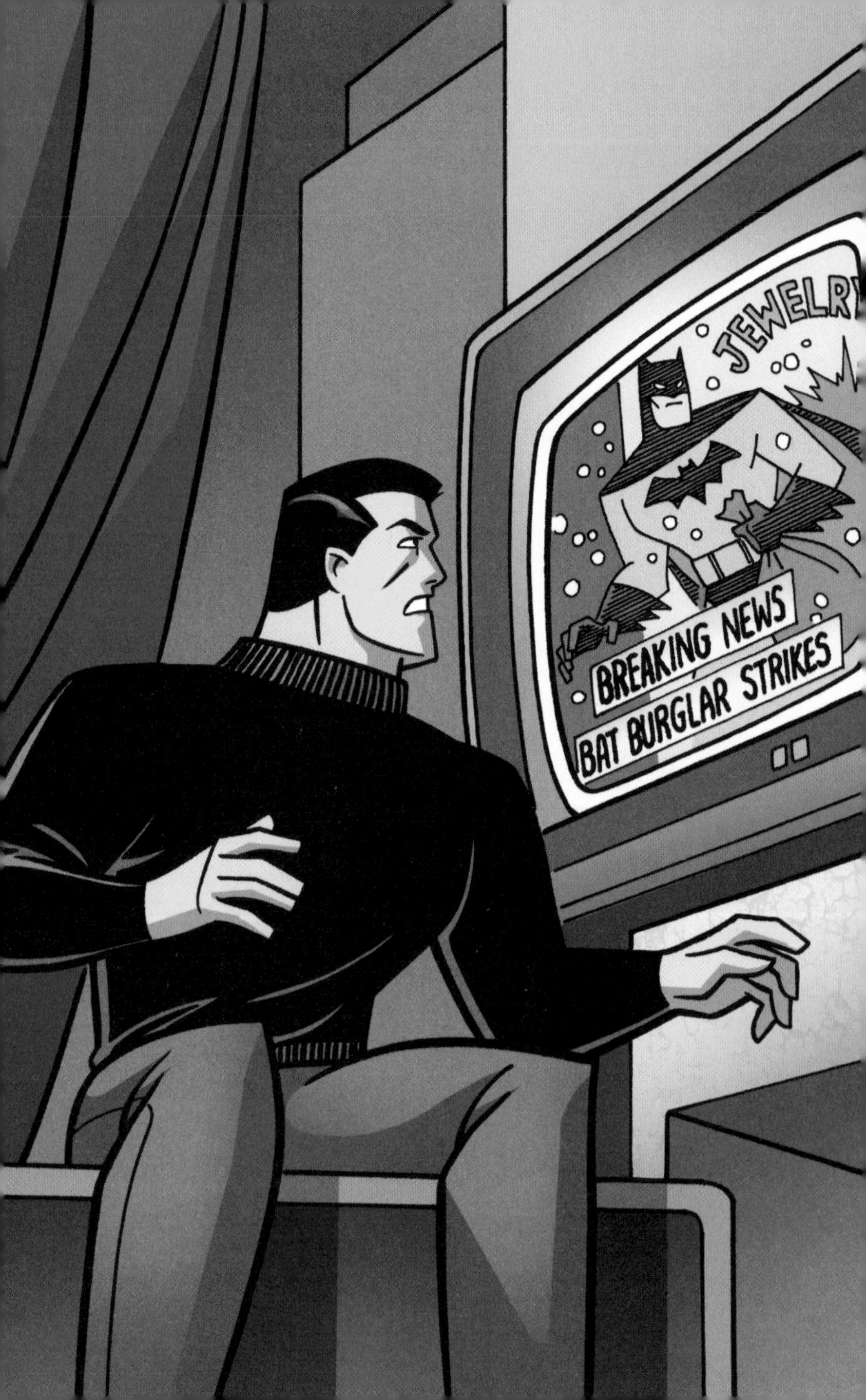
JEWELRY
BREAKING NEWS
BAT BURGLAR STRIKES

Then suddenly, the camera angle switched again. The tape showed Batman holding a garbage bag full of jewels. A moment later, the police officers burst through the door. "Batman! He's stealing my jewels!" screamed the store owner. On the video, Batman raised his hands into the air. "You've caught me, boys," he said. "Now, if you'll excuse me —"

As Batman fled out the rear door of store, the tape ended.

Spring O'Hara continued her report. "Has the Dark Knight switched to the dark side? Is the Caped Crusader really a caped crook?" she asked. "As always, Channel 12 will keep you updated as more information becomes available. For now, we'll continue our regularly scheduled program, *Birds of the Serengeti*."

Bruce rose from his chair. "What's going on?!" he said. "That's not what happened. The tape didn't even show the real thief!"

"Is everything all right, Master Bruce?" asked Alfred from the doorway. He entered the room, pushing a breakfast cart with a covered serving tray on top.

"Have you seen this, Alfred?" said Bruce, pointing toward the television screen.

"Why, yes," he replied. "There's a lovely piece on the Serengeti's spotted woodpecker."

"No," Bruce interrupted. "The news reports. They're blaming Batman for last night's robbery. They've edited the security tapes to make me look like the crook."

"Perhaps you should sit down, sir," said Alfred. He lifted the lid of the serving tray.

Bruce looked down at the cart of food, coffee, and the daily paper. "I'm in no mood for breakfast," he said.

"And rightfully so, sir," said Alfred. He gently nudged the newspaper toward his boss. The morning headline covered the front page in thick, bold print:

THE THIEF WEARS A MASK!

Bruce snatched the paper from the cart and started reading. "Don Russo, owner of Don's Diamond Store, was held at gunpoint last night during an attempted robbery," he began. "When asked if he could identify the assailant, Russo replied, 'No, but the thief was wearing a dark, black mask.'"

Bruce looked at the small image next to the article. It was a photo of Batman, and the newspaper had added an arrow pointing to his dark, black cowl.

"You said yourself that reporters never get anything right," Alfred suggested.

"This isn't a simple mistake, Alfred," Bruce shouted. "They're twisting the truth!"

"There's something you should know, sir," Alfred said. He pointed to the top of the newspaper's front page.

"The *Penguin Times!*" exclaimed Bruce, noticing the paper's new name. "What happened to the *Gotham Gazette*?"

Meanwhile, across town at the newly named Air Penguin Broadcasting Studios, Spring O'Hara stormed out of the newsroom. "I won't do it," she yelled, picking up her briefcase and heading for the studio's door. "I never liked Batman, but I'm a journalist. It's my job to seek the truth and report it, not lie to our viewers."

"Is that what you think we're doing?" asked the Penguin. He stood on the other side of the doorway, twirling an umbrella.

"Mr. Cobblepot, I, uh," O'Hara stuttered, and then bravely spoke up. "Well, yes, we're lying to the public. You know that Batman didn't commit these crimes."

Penguin chuckled, pacing in front of the nervous reporter. "Did you know, Ms. O'Hara," he began, "that most birds can't move their eyes from side to side?"

O'Hara stared at the pudgy man in front of her. She clutched her briefcase to her chest, now slightly frightened and confused. "No," she replied.

"It's true," he continued. "Birds only see what's directly in front of their face. Unless, of course, they choose to turn their head."

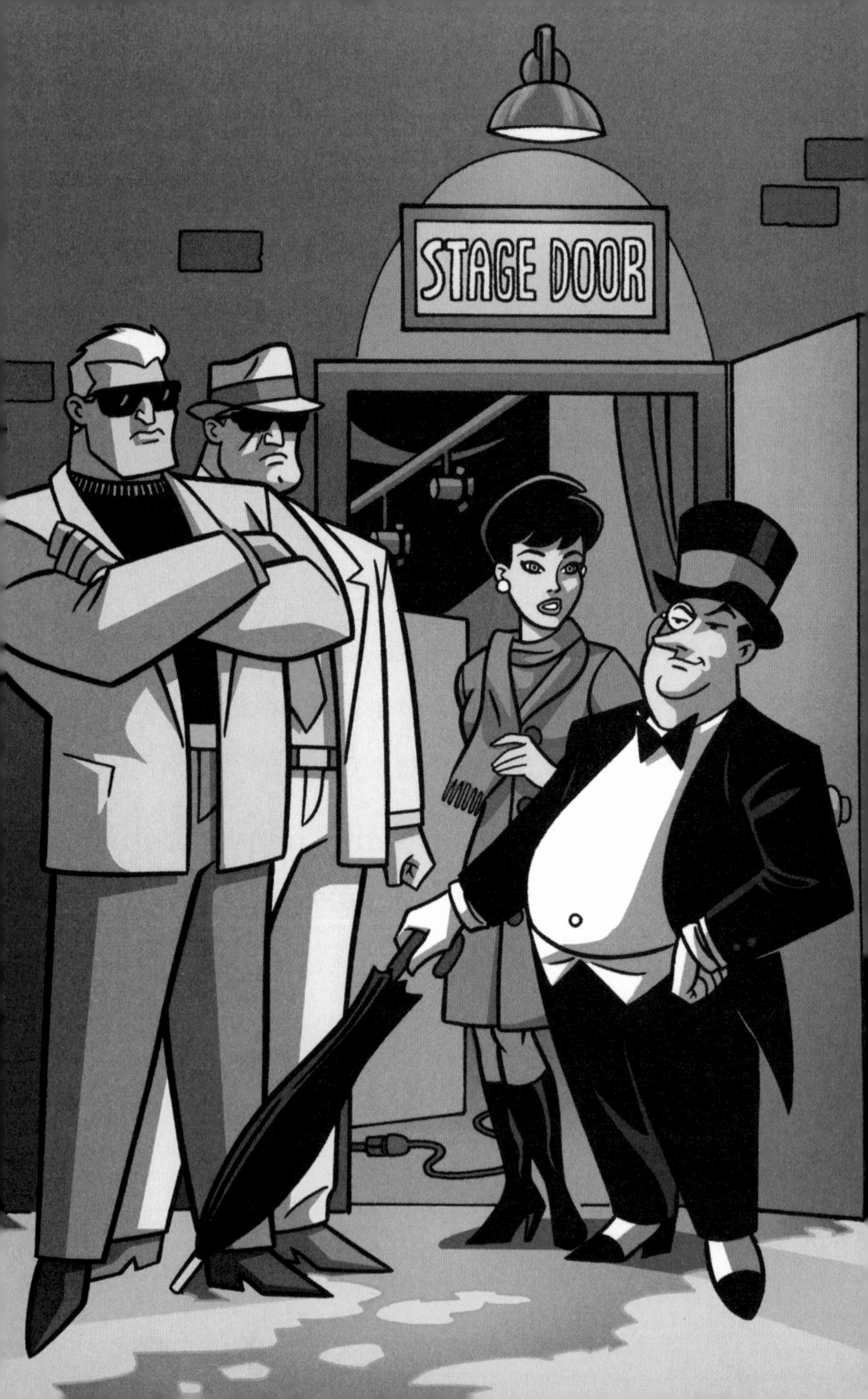
STAGE DOOR

"What are you saying?" asked O'Hara.

"Birds and humans aren't all that different, you see," answered Penguin. "I show the public one version of the truth, but they have the choice to look away."

"Well, find somebody else to feed them your lies," she shouted. "I quit!"

O'Hara walked past Penguin toward the exit. Suddenly, two large goons in suits appeared in the doorway, blocking her way. The men crossed their arms. They stared down angrily at the reporter through their dark sunglasses.

"Let me go!" O'Hara screamed.

"And another thing, Ms. O'Hara," said the Penguin. "Even the strongest chick can fall prey to a larger bird."

CHAPTER 4

THE CRIME BIRD SINGS

A few miles away, the Batmobile raced toward Gotham. Batman knew that the Penguin was responsible for the phony news reports. He had to stop the crook and end the lies before they grew any worse.

Driving over the Trigate Bridge, Batman flicked on the radio for the latest updates. "We're live at City Hall," a news reporter began. "More than 2,000 angry citizens have gathered, demanding Batman's capture. Mayor Hamilton Hill has come out to address the crowd. Let's listen in . . ."

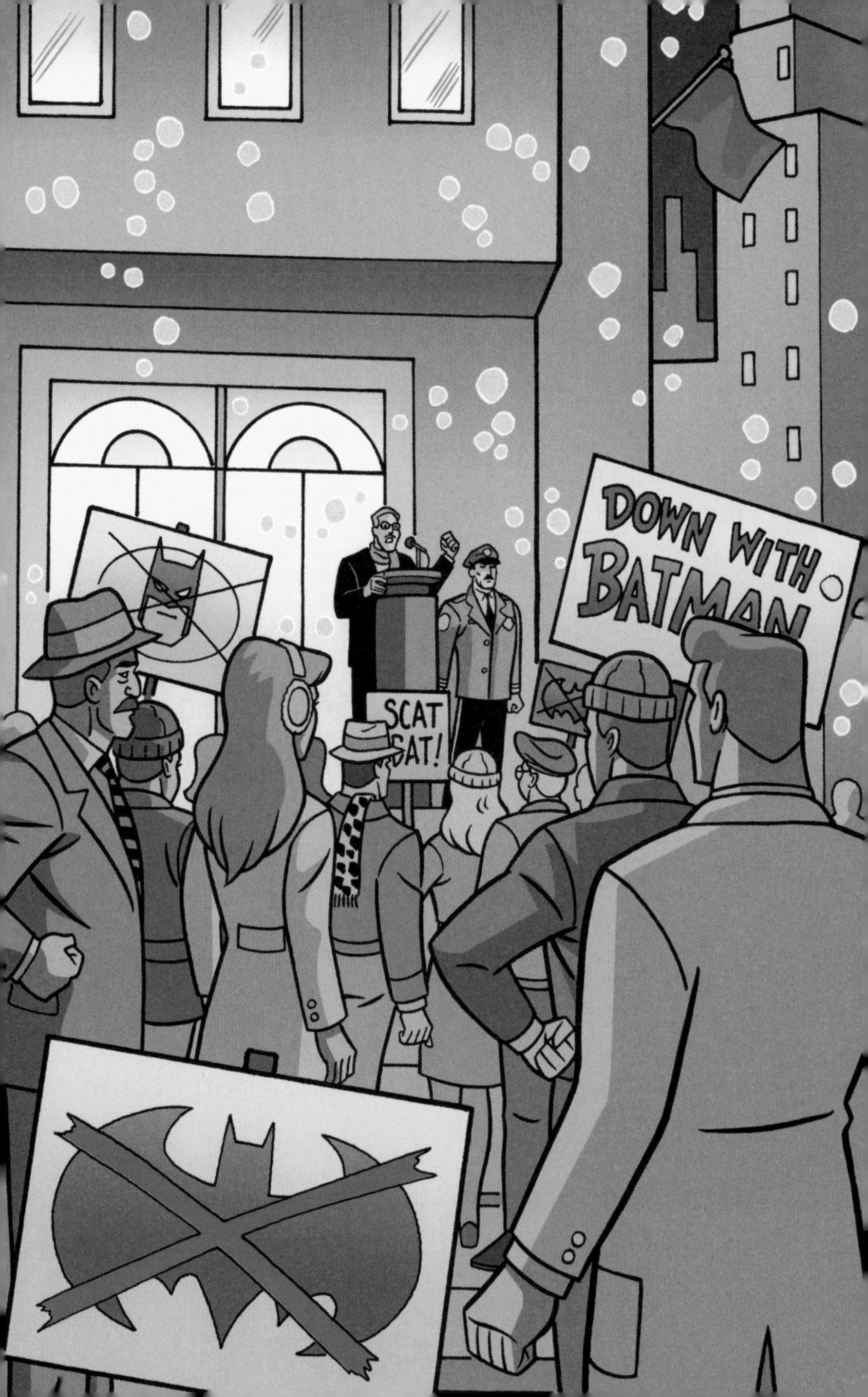
DOWN WITH BATMAN
SCAT BAT!

"Good afternoon, fellow citizens of Gotham," said Mayor Hill. "I want to assure you all that this matter will be handled swiftly. No man is above the law in our fair city, and that includes Batman!"

Suddenly, a light on the Batmobile's dashboard lit up, signaling an incoming call. Batman turned down the radio. "Activate phone," he commanded.

"This is Commissioner Gordon," said a voice on the other end. "Where are you?" Gordon's voice was nearly drowned out by what sounded like a roaring crowd.

"Where are *you*?" Batman asked. "I can barely hear you speak."

"City Hall," Gordon replied. "Don't come down here. This crowd is getting out of control. They want your head on a platter."

"What about you, Jim?" asked Batman. "Do you believe in the Bat Burglar?"

"You know I don't watch the news," he replied. "I see the real stories every day on the streets."

Over the phone, Batman could hear the angry chants of the crowd in the background. "No more Batman! No more Batman!" they shouted.

"I'll tell you something else," the commissioner continued. "A few boys on the force would love to see you taken down. Until this thing blows over, Batman, you need to be careful."

"So, what else is new?" Batman growled. He clicked off the Batmobile's phone, turned on the afterburners, and sped off in search of the Penguin.

Back at Air Penguin Studios, *Channel 12 News* was five minutes from their nightly broadcast. Spring O'Hara sat behind the anchor's desk, surrounded by video cameras. Penguin had already let the crew and other news workers go. O'Hara shuffled through a stack of papers, nervously preparing to report the day's top stories.

"Stick to the script," said the Penguin. He circled around O'Hara, hovering over her like a hawk.

"You can't make me do this!" she shouted. "You can't make me report these lies about Batman!"

"Then maybe our viewers would be interested in the lies you've already told," replied the Penguin. "The public isn't quick to forgive. I can assure you, Ms. O'Hara, your reporting days would soon be over."

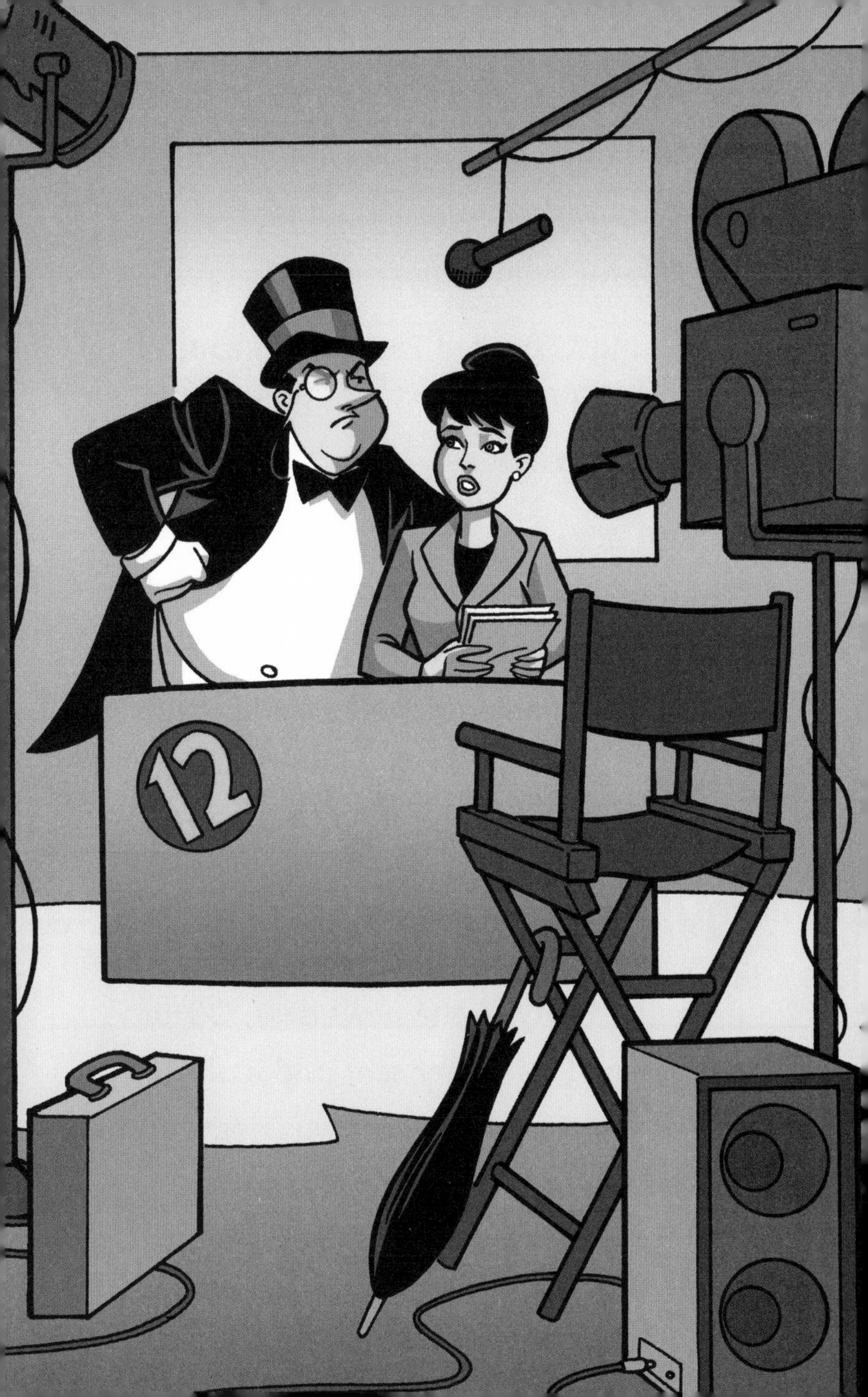
12

"But you tricked me," said O'Hara. "I didn't know they were lies, at first. The viewers will believe me."

"Wrong!" shouted Penguin. "I control the media. I am Gotham's only truth. They will believe *me*!"

"Still not convinced?" asked the Penguin. "Well, maybe you'll listen to my goons." He pointed to the two large men dressed in suits and ties standing behind the video cameras. Both goons gave an evil grin. "One slip of the tongue, Ms. O'Hara, and it's bye-bye birdie!" said Penguin.

WHAM! The Penguin slammed his umbrella down on the news desk. O'Hara straightened up in her seat and looked toward the cameras. There was nothing she could do.

"Now get ready!" the Penguin shouted. "We go live on the air in ninety seconds."

"Then I'm just in time for the show," came a voice from the studio's doorway.

The Penguin twirled around. A shadowy figure entered the room. "Why, if it isn't the Bat Burglar himself," he said. "We were just talking about you."

"Nothing bad, I hope," said Batman.

"You'll have to watch the news and find out," answered the Penguin.

Batman advanced toward the Penguin. "I'm afraid tonight's broadcast has been canceled," he said.

"Ha! Our ratings have never been better," shouted the Penguin. "You're the one who's finished. Get him, boys!"

The Penguin's goons rushed toward Batman. The Dark Knight swiftly removed a blow-gun from his Utility Belt. *PHWOOT!* *PHWOOT!* He fired two small pellets toward the approaching men. The pellets hit the goons before they could react. The pellets splattered into a sticky film, which covered each of their faces.

The goons mumbled for help. They clawed at their mouths and eyes, but the sticky goo wouldn't come off.

Batman grabbed a Batarang from his belt. The metal weapon was attached to a wire. He spun it around his head like a lasso. With one quick snap of the wrist, he flung the Batarang toward the flailing goons. It whizzed around the men, tangling them in loops of super-strong wire.

"Show's over, Penguin," said Batman.

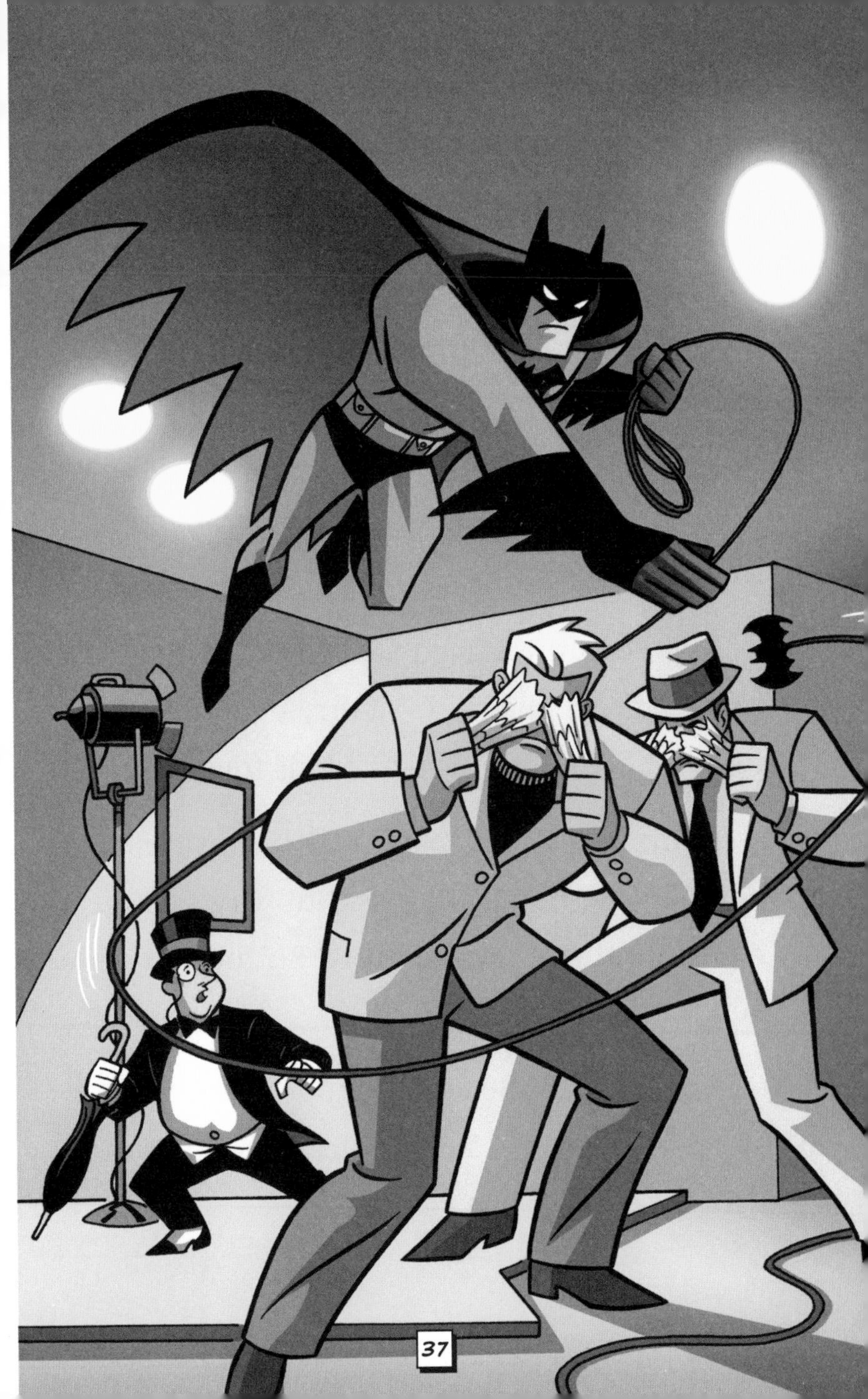

"Wrong again, Batman," said the Penguin. "This fat bird has yet to sing."

The Penguin pointed his umbrella toward Batman and pressed a hidden trigger on its handle. **RAT·TAT·TAT!** Bullets exploded from the umbrella's tip. Batman dove to the side as shots sprayed the wall behind him.

The Penguin moved toward Batman. "That's right," he said. "Scurry away, you pesky rat! You're finished in this town!"

Batman glanced toward O'Hara, sitting alone at the news desk. "Is that why you're reporting these lies?" shouted Batman at Penguin. "To get rid of me?"

The pudgy little crook stopped firing his secret weapon. He stood in front of Batman with an evil grin on his face.

"You're not as dumb as you look, Batman," replied the Penguin, "With you out of the way, I will rule this town. Everyone knows those clumsy cops couldn't catch a cold without you."

"And you knew the public would turn against me?" prodded Batman.

"Of course, the people of Gotham will believe anything they see on TV," said the Penguin. "They're nothing but a bunch of lazy, brainless, couch potatoes —"

". . . brainless, couch potatoes . . ." Penguin's voice echoed through the room.

"What?" said the puzzled crook, spinning toward the sound of the echo.

Above the news desk, the Penguin saw a giant image of himself on the studio's television monitor.

"What's going on?" Penguin shouted. Then he noticed the empty chair where Spring O'Hara had been sitting.

"Over here!" yelled the reporter, waving from behind one of the video cameras. She had turned on the camera, pointing it in the direction of the Penguin and Batman. "I guess the show's over now, huh, Penguin?" she said. "Because you just sang to all of Gotham's ten million viewers."

CHAPTER 5

THE SHOW'S OVER

"Blasted! Fooled by a bird with a brain!" yelled the Penguin. "Sadly, I can't stick around for the final credits."

RAT·TAT·TAT! The Penguin fired his umbrella into the air. Shards of wood and steel fell from the ceiling. Nothing was left but a gaping hole, showing the open sky.

"Ta-ta!" said the Penguin. He flipped another switch on the umbrella. It snapped open and started spinning like a helicopter blade. The Penguin soared into the air and through the hole in the ceiling.

"Not so fast," shouted Batman. He grabbed the grappling-hook launcher from his Utility Belt. He pointed it into the air and fired. **POW!** The launcher shot a metal hook toward the escaping crook. As the hook flew upward, a line of super-strong wire unraveled behind it.

Just before the Penguin flew out of sight, the metal hook clamped onto the umbrella's handle. **WHOOOOSH!** Batman was yanked into the air through the hole in the ceiling. He dangled below the umbrella, holding tightly to the grappling-hook launcher.

"Batman!" yelled the Penguin. They flew higher into the air, hovering over downtown Gotham City.

Batman gripped the launcher even tighter. A cold rain pelted his face and froze instantly onto his Batsuit.

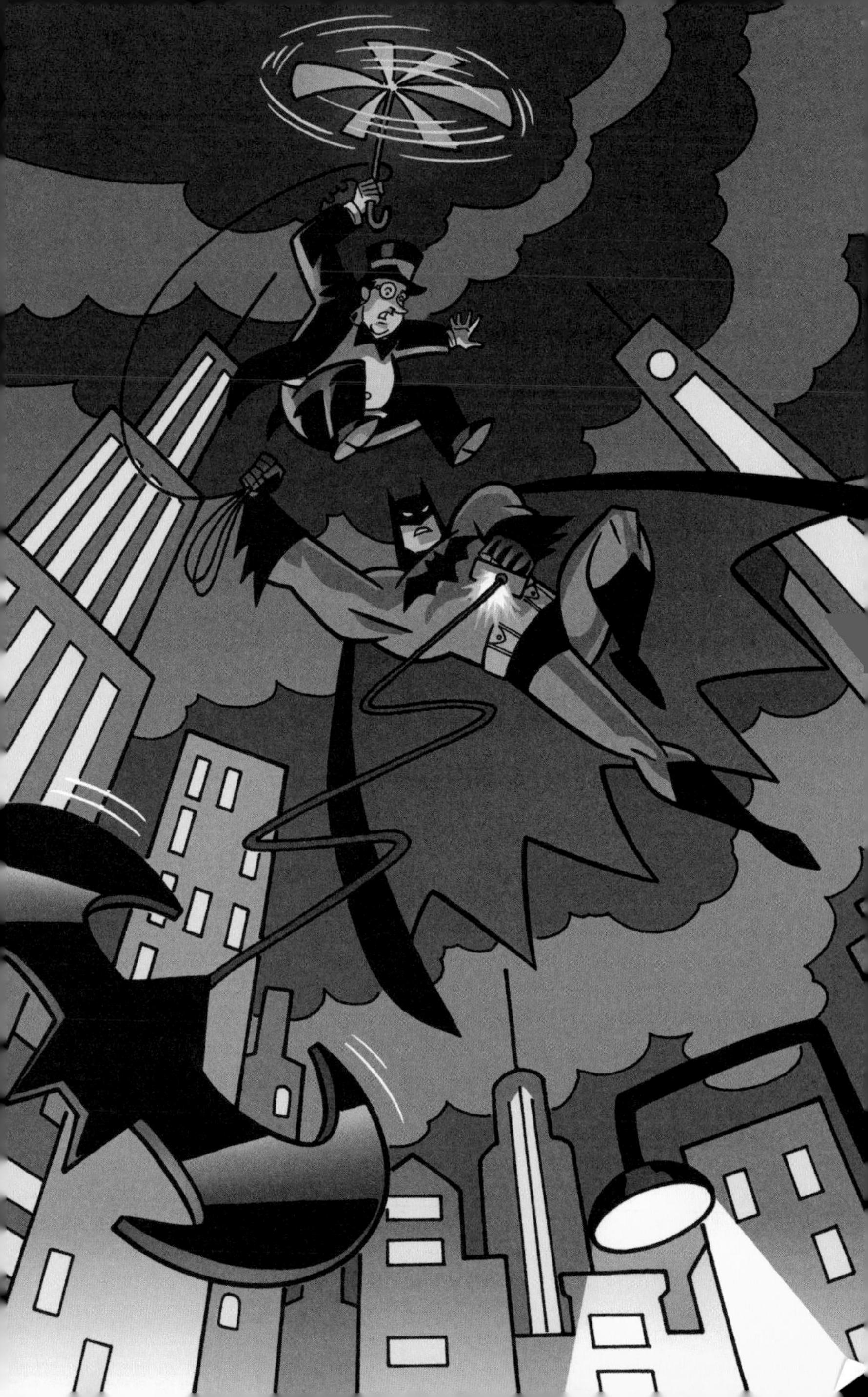

"Say, Cobblepot," Batman yelled upward. "Didn't anyone ever tell you that penguins can't fly?"

With one hand, Batman grabbed a second grappling-hook launcher from his Utility Belt and fired it at the ground below. **KKLLAAAANG!** The hook wedged into the concrete sidewalk along Murphy Avenue. Dozens of pedestrians scattered at the sight.

The Penguin's umbrella suddenly jerked to a stop. "Hey," yelled the crook. "Let me go!" He increased the power on his umbrella, trying to free himself from Batman's grasp.

Batman groaned. His arms stretched in opposite directions. He struggled to hold on. **SNAP** The wire attached to the ground suddenly snapped like a rubber band.

Batman and the Penguin shot through the air. They arced upward and then spiraled downward, unable to stop themselves. Before they hit the ground, Batman grabbed Penguin. He sheltered the crook beneath his cape.

WHAM! Both men slammed onto the downtown sidewalk.

"Ugh," moaned Batman. He picked himself up from the sidewalk. His cape was partially torn and his face was scraped from the fall. His armored suit had saved his life and spared him any broken bones. Nearby, the Penguin struggled to get to his feet.

Then, just as both men began to recover, an angry crowd stomped toward them. Both Batman and Penguin stood, watching as they approached.

Suddenly, a policeman in the crowd yelled to the Penguin, "Clumsy, eh?" Another mob member shouted, "Brainless couch potatoes, huh? We'll see about that!"

The crowd chased Penguin down the street. "I'll get you for this, Batman!" he yelled. "I'll get you!"

"The public isn't quick to forgive," Batman said. He knew that true justice would be served.

The next morning, Bruce returned to Wayne Manor. The exhausted billionaire quickly removed the Batsuit. Then he stepped into a long, hot shower.

Afterward, Bruce dried off and slipped into his bathrobe. Steam from the shower had fogged up the bathroom mirrors. He opened the nearby window.

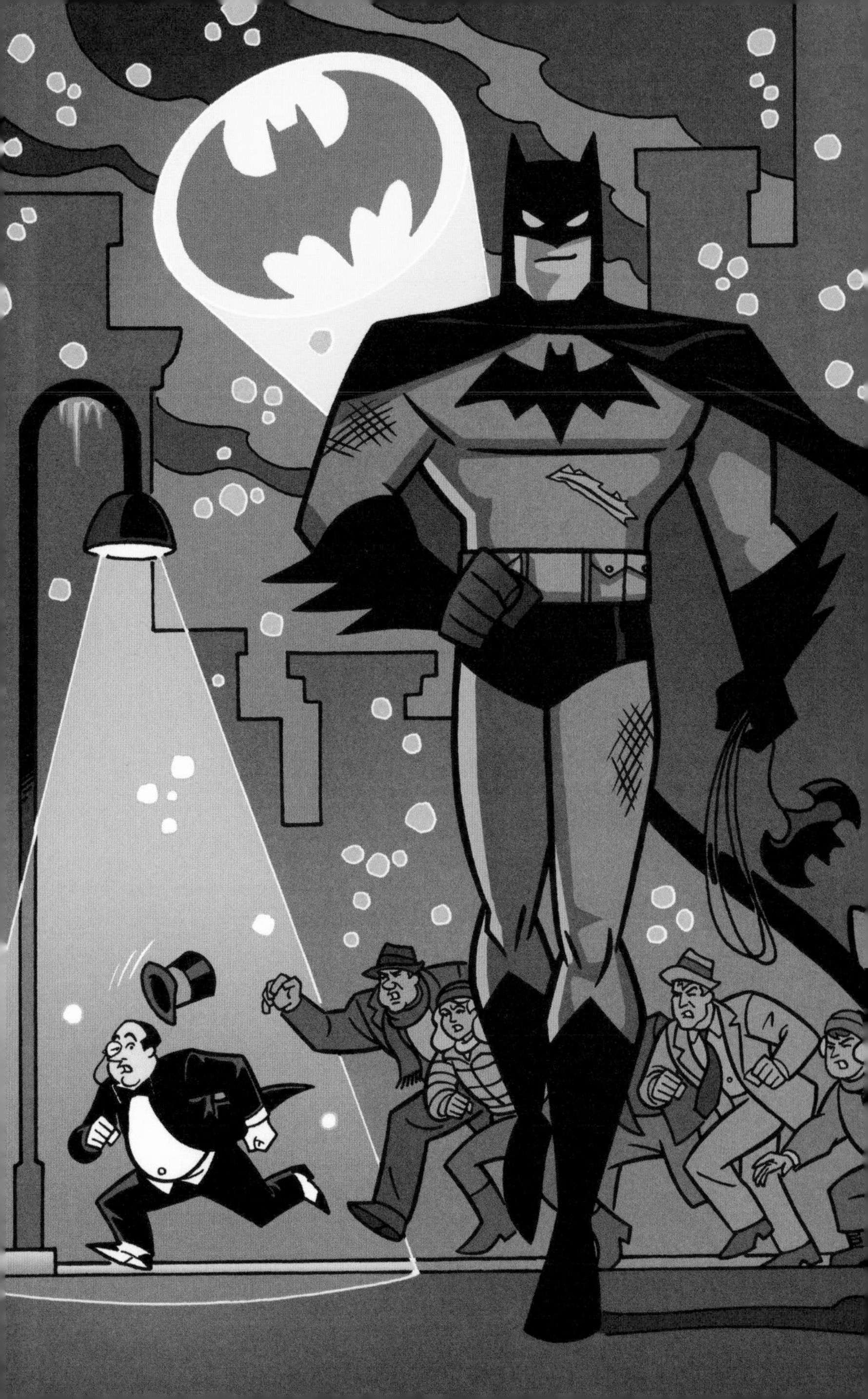

"Ah," Bruce said, as the morning air blew into the room. "Maybe the weather is starting to warm up after all."

After bandaging his wounds, Bruce returned to the sitting room. He plopped into his chair. Ready to relax in front of the television, Bruce reached for the remote.

"Huh?" he said, looking over at the end table. The television remote was gone, replaced by a tall stack of books. "Alfred," Bruce shouted toward the doorway.

The loyal butler promptly entered the room. "You called, sir?" he asked.

Bruce placed his hand atop the stack of books. He gave Alfred a questioning look.

"The books, of course!" exclaimed Alfred. "Well, I thought we could use a bit of a change around here."

Bruce glanced at the blank television screen. "Perhaps you're right, Alfred," he replied.

"If that'll be all, sir," Alfred said, turning to leave.

"One more thing," said Bruce. He held up a large book from the stack, *A Step-by-Step Guide to Bird Watching.* "Don't you think we've seen enough birds for a while?"

Alfred turned back and smiled. "That's the North American edition," he said. "I can assure you, sir, that book doesn't contain a single penguin."

Penguin, The

REAL NAME: Oswald Cobblepot

OCCUPATION: Professional Criminal

BASE: Gotham City

HEIGHT:
5 feet 2 inches

WEIGHT:
175 pounds

EYES:
Blue

HAIR:
Black

Like the flightless fowl he resembles, Oswald Cobblepot has little skill in combat and doesn't seem very threatening. He is, however, a dangerous criminal mastermind constantly in search of easy money. Although he is one of the wealthiest men in Gotham, few of the Penguin's dollar bills have come from honest sources. Expect the Penguin to be protected at all times by a group of hired muscle.

G.C.P.D. GOTHAM CITY POLICE DEPARTMENT

- Cobblepot's waddling walk and beakish nose earned him the unwanted nickname "Penguin." His pursuit of wealth and success comes from the desire to rise above those who have teased him.

- The Penguin operates out of his fashionable nightclub, the Iceberg Lounge, which serves as a safe haven for crafty crooks of all kinds. While there, he spreads his wings in order to connect with the criminal elite.

- The Penguin has a number of tricks up his sleeve. His special umbrellas can hide a variety of deadly tools, including a machine gun, a flamethrower, or a blade. They can also double as a parachute or helicopter, allowing him to fly away from situations gone afoul.

- Penguin has an obsession with birds. He often chooses his crimes so they connect with a bird theme in some way. On more than one occasion, he has used carrier pigeons to send criminal messages.

CONFIDENTIAL

BIOGRAPHIES

Donald Lemke works as a children's book editor. He is the author of the Zinc Alloy graphic novel series. He also wrote *Captured Off Guard*, a World War II story, and a graphic novelization of *Gulliver's Travels*, both selected by the Junior Library Guild.

Erik Doescher is an illustrator and video game designer based in Dallas, Texas. He attended the School of Visual Arts in New York City. Erik illustrated for a number of comic studios, and then moved to Texas to pursue videogame development and design. However, he has not given up on illustrating his favorite comic book characters.

Mike DeCarlo is a longtime contributor of comic art whose range extends from Batman and Iron Man to Bugs Bunny and Scooby-Doo. He resides in Connecticut with his wife and four children.

Lee Loughridge has been working in comics for over 14 years. He currently lives in sunny California in a tent on the beach.

GLOSSARY

afterburners (AF-tur-bur-nerz)—devices used to increase the speed of something

assailant (uh-SEY-luhnt)—an attacker

cavern (KAV-ern)—a large cave

courtyard (KORT-yard)—an open area surrounded by walls

evidence (EV-uh-duhnss)—information and facts that help prove something

flailing (FLEYL-ing)—waving or swinging your arms quickly and desperately

flurry (FLUR-ee)—a sudden burst

fowl (FOUL)—a bird

phony (FOH-nee)—not real or genuine

spiraled (SPYE-ruhld)—circled

Utility Belt (yoo-TIL-uh-tee BELT)—Batman's belt, which holds all of his weaponry and gadgets

DISCUSSION QUESTIONS

1. The Penguin twists the truth when he reports the news. Do you think the media ever tell lies? What are some ways to tell if a story is true or false?

2. Billionaire Bruce Wayne's secret identity is Batman. Do you think Bruce should tell others about his secret identity? Why or why not?

3. Alfred tells Bruce to stop watching TV for a while so he can read more books. Which do you think is better — reading or television? Explain.

WRITING PROMPTS

1. If you ran a TV news station, what type of news would you cover? Write a news report, then think up a catchy headline for it.

2. The Penguin is a bird fanatic. What are some of your hobbies and interests? What things are you extremely interested in?

3. Graphic novels are often illustrated and written by different people. Write a comic book of your own. Then have a friend illustrate it for you.

MORE NEW BATMAN ADVENTURES!

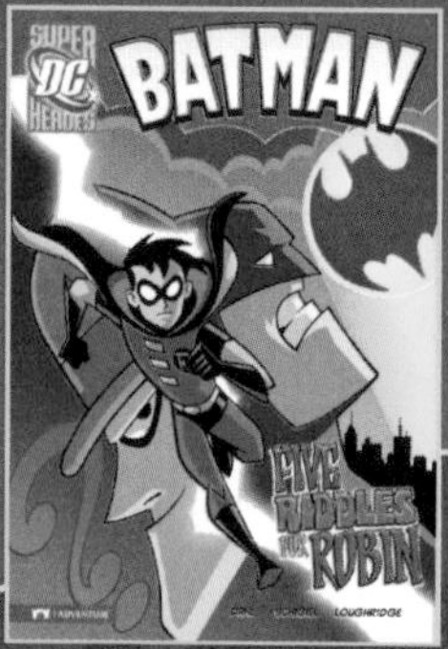
SUPER DC HEROES
BATMAN
FIVE RIDDLES FOR ROBIN

FIVE RIDDLES FOR ROBIN

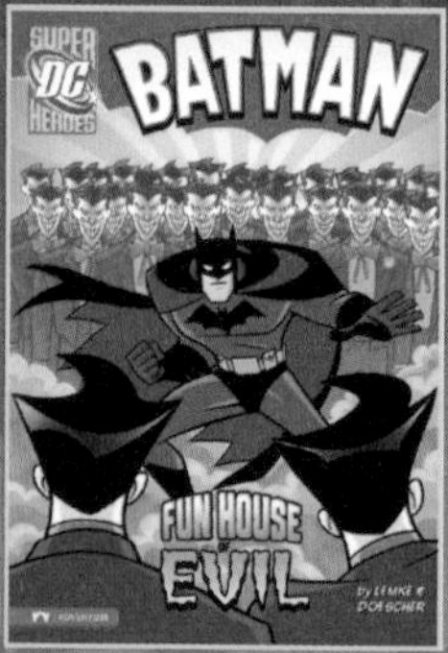
SUPER DC HEROES
BATMAN
FUN HOUSE OF EVIL

FUN HOUSE OF EVIL

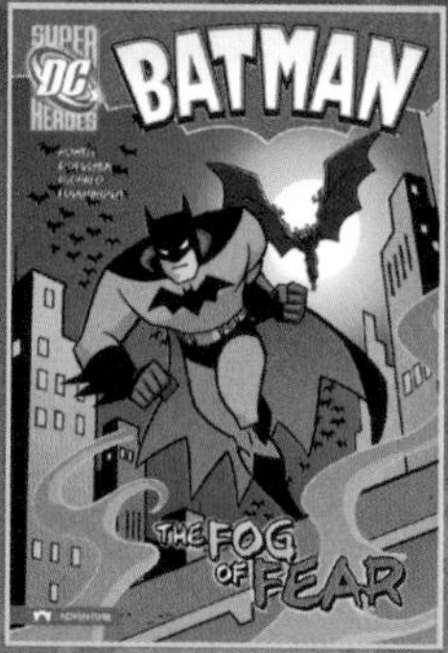
SUPER DC HEROES
BATMAN
THE FOG OF FEAR

THE FOG OF FEAR

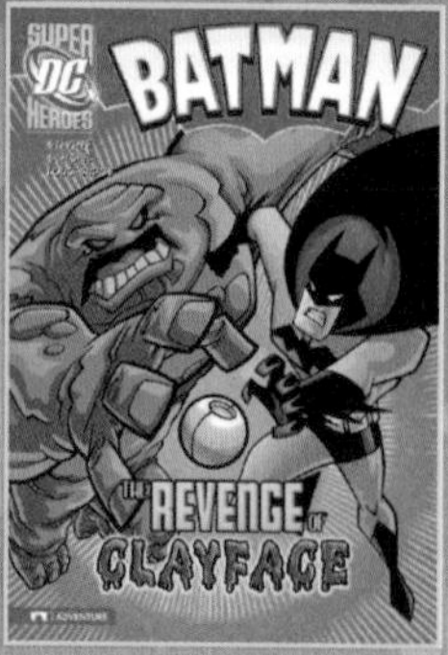
SUPER DC HEROES
BATMAN
THE REVENGE OF CLAYFACE

THE REVENGE OF CLAYFACE

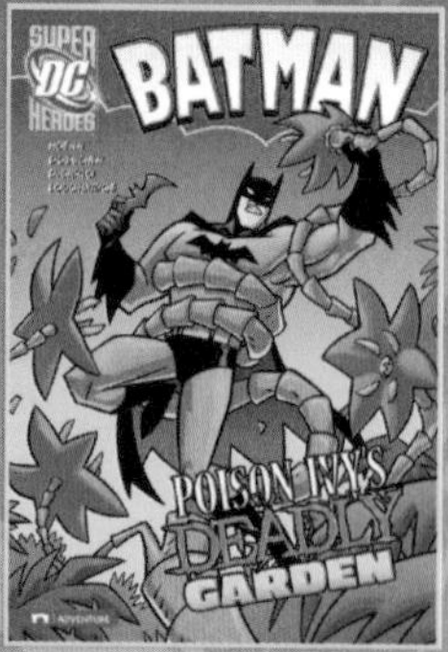
SUPER DC HEROES
BATMAN
POISON IVY'S DEADLY GARDEN

POISON IVY'S DEADLY GARDEN

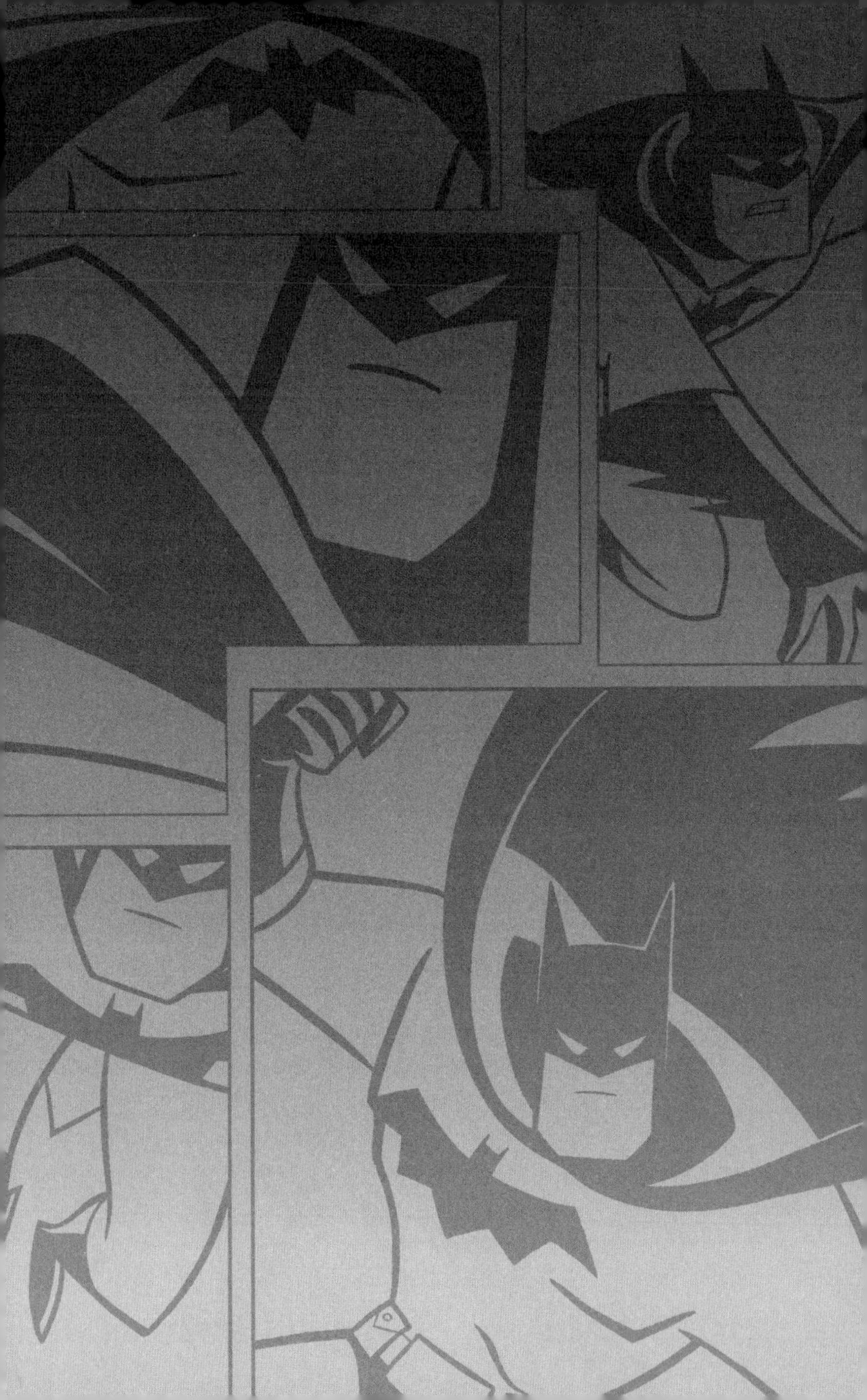

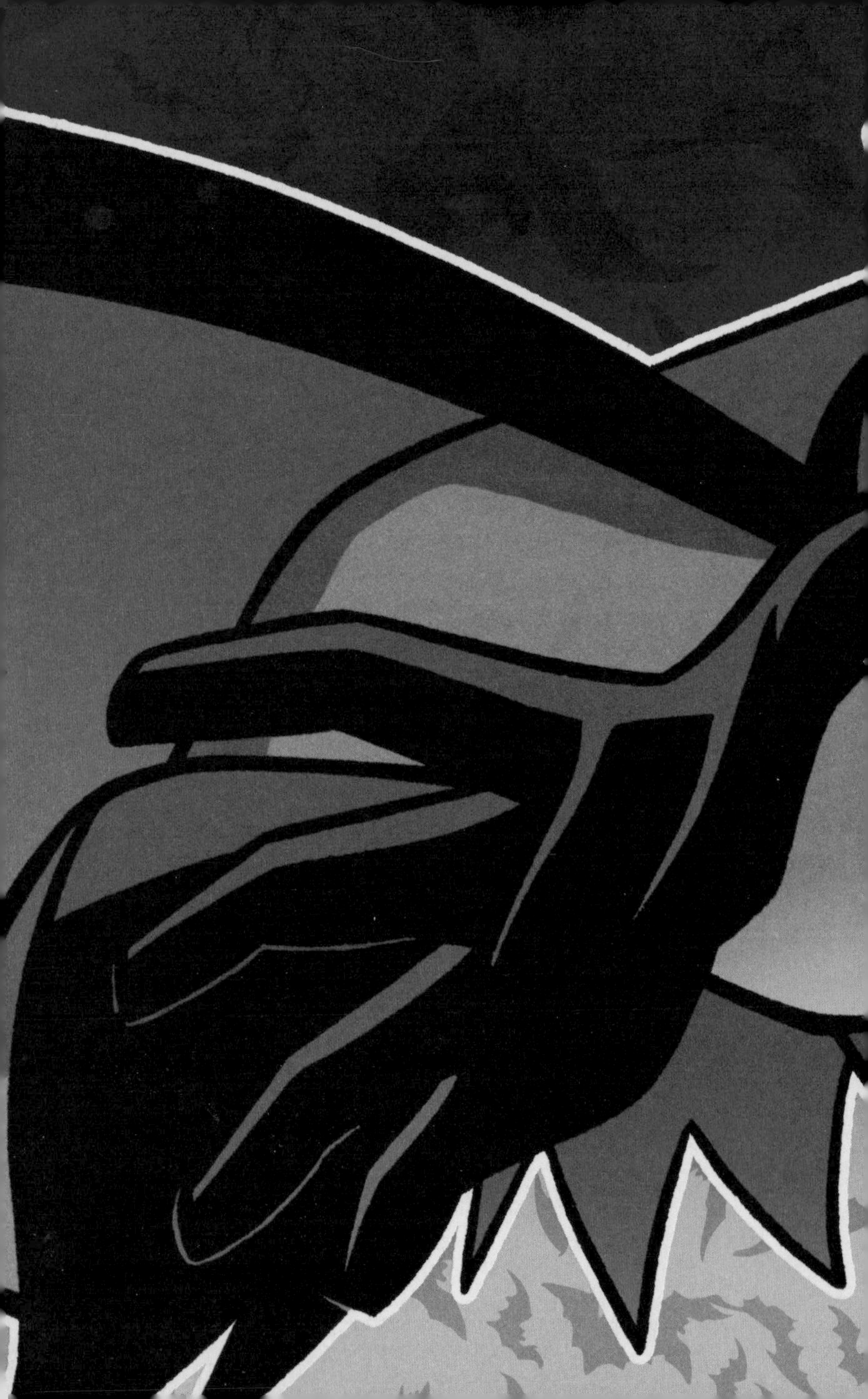